Mis deportes favoritos / My Favorite Sports

ME ENCANTA EL BALONCESTO/
I LOVE BASKETBALL

By Ryan Nagelhout   Traducido por Eida de la Vega

Please visit our website, www.garethstevens.com. For a free color catalog of all our high-quality books, call toll free 1-800-542-2595 or fax 1-877-542-2596.

Library of Congress Cataloging-in-Publication Data

Nagelhout, Ryan.
I love basketball = Me encanta el baloncesto / by Ryan Nagelhout.
 p. cm. — (My favorite sports = Mis deportes favoritos)
Parallel title: Mis deportes favoritos
In English and Spanish.
Includes index.
ISBN 978-1-4824-0848-5 (library binding)
1. Basketball — United States — Juvenile literature. I. Nagelhout, Ryan. II. Title.
GV885.1 N34 2015
796.323—d23

First Edition

Published in 2015 by
Gareth Stevens Publishing
111 East 14th Street, Suite 349
New York, NY 10003

Copyright © 2015 Gareth Stevens Publishing

Editor: Ryan Nagelhout
Designer: Nick Domiano
Spanish Translation: Eida de la Vega

Photo credits: Cover, pp. 1 rskin/iStock/Thinkstock.com; p. 5 Wealan Pollard/OJO Images/Getty Images; p. 7 Fuse/Thinkstock.com; pp. 17, 24 (pass) Jami Garrison/Shutterstock.com; pp. 9, 13, 24 (uniform) Brand X Pictures/Thinkstock.com; p. 11 Hyperion Pixels/iStock/Thinkstock.com; p. 15 bst2012/iStock/Thinkstock.com; p. 19 Stefano Lunardi/iStock/Thinkstock.com; pp. 21, 24 (net) TaMaNKunGf/Shutterstock.com; p. 23 Mike Kemp/Blend Images/Getty Images.

All rights reserved. No part of this book may be reproduced in any form without permission in writing from the publisher, except by a reviewer.

Printed in the United States of America

CPSIA compliance information: Batch #CS15GS: For further information contact Gareth Stevens, New York, New York at 1-800-542-2595.

Contenido

Pasión por el baloncesto. 4

Botar la pelota. 14

¡Pásala!. 16

¡Buen tiro!. 20

Palabras que debes saber. 24

Índice 24

Contents

Basketball Love. 4

Bouncing Ball. 14

Pass It!. 16

Good Shot!. 20

Words to Know 24

Index. 24

¡El baloncesto
es divertido!

Basketball is fun!

Juego con mis amigos.

I play it with my friends.

Juego en un equipo.

I play on a team.

Casi todas las pelotas son de caucho. Algunas son de cuero.

Most basketballs are rubber. Some are made of leather.

La ropa que usa el equipo es toda igual. Es un uniforme.

My team wears the same clothes. This is called a uniform.

Me gusta botar
la pelota.

I love to bounce
the ball.

Se la paso a mi amigo.

I pass it to my friend.

Me gusta lanzar
a la canasta.

I like to shoot at a net.

Conseguí meterla en la canasta. A eso se le llama encestar.

I made it in the hoop. A made shot is called a basket.

¡Ganamos el juego!

My team won the game!

Palabras que debes saber/ Words to Know

la canasta/ net

pasar/ pass

el uniforme/ uniform

Índice / Index

canasta/net 18

encestar/basket 20

equipo/team 8, 12

uniforme/uniform 12